This Walker book belongs to:

·····························

·····························

·····························

For Rufus ♥

First published 2005 by Walker Books Ltd
87 Vauxhall Walk, London SE11 5HJ

This edition published 2013

10

Lucy Cousins © 2005

The right of Lucy Cousins to be identified as author/illustrator of this work
has been asserted by her in accordance with the Copyright, Designs and Patents Act 1988

This book was hand lettered by Lucy Cousins

Printed in China

British Library Cataloguing in Publication Data:
a catalogue record for this book is available from the British Library

ISBN 978-1-4063-4501-8

www.walker.co.uk

Hooray for Fish!

Lucy Cousins

WALKER BOOKS
AND SUBSIDIARIES
LONDON • BOSTON • SYDNEY • AUCKLAND

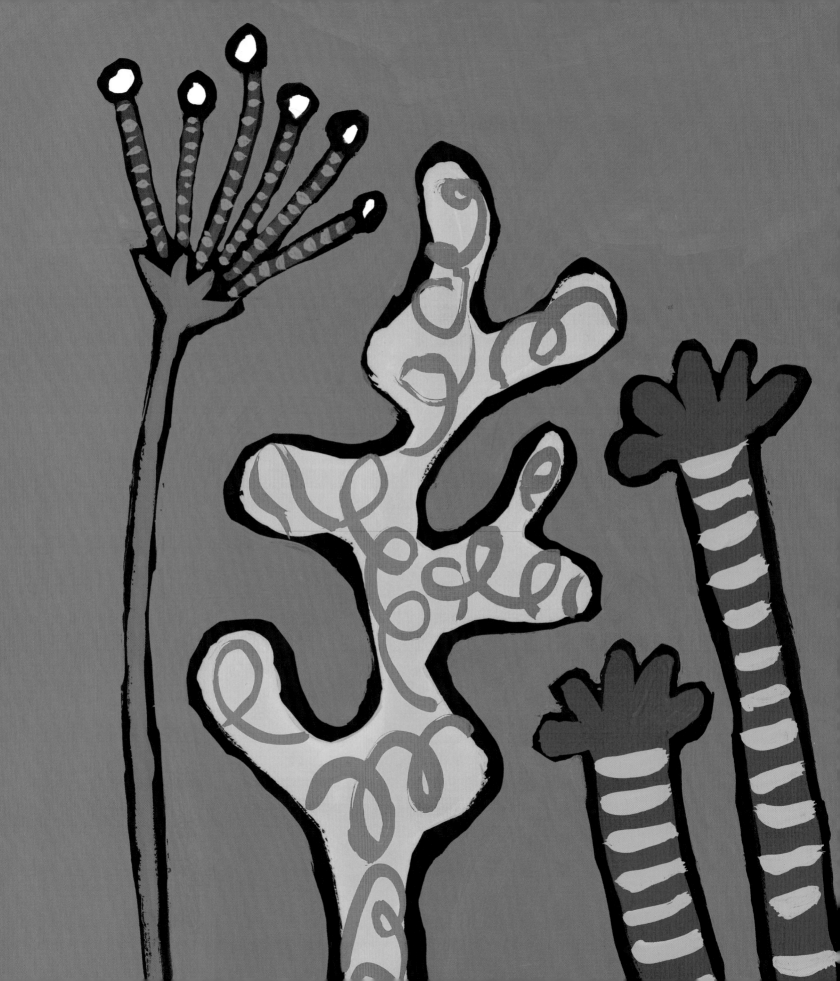

Hello! I am Little Fish,
swimming in the sea.
I have lots of fishy friends.
Come along with
me.

Hello, hello, hello, fish,

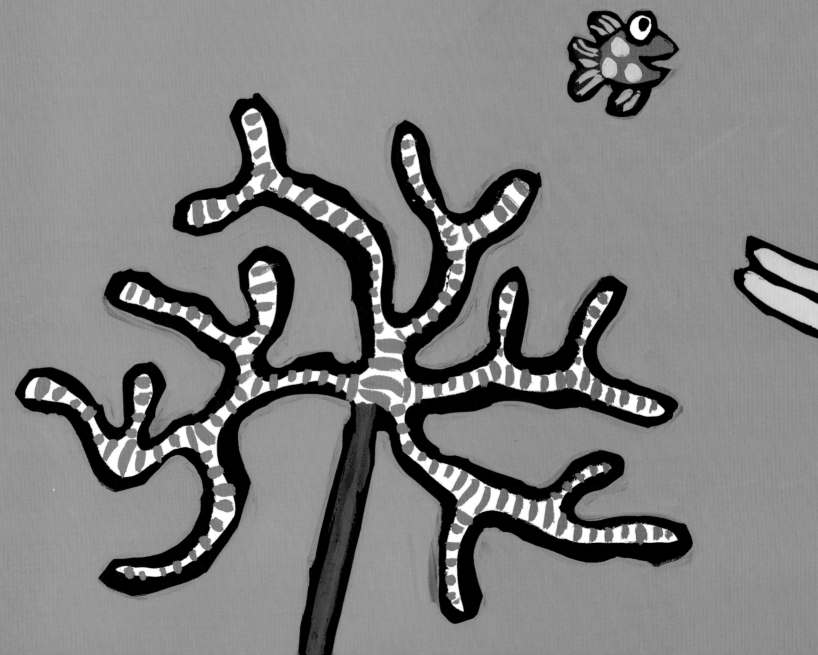

red,
blue

and yellow fish.

Hello, spotty fish,

stripy fish,

happy fish,

grumpy fish.

How many can you see?

Hello, ele-fish,

shelly
fish.

Hello,
hairy fish,

eye fish,

shy fish,

Hello,
fat and
thin fish.

Hello, twin

fin-fin fish.

Curly whirly,

twisty twirly,

upside
down,

round and round.

So many friends,

so many
fish,

splosh, splash, Splish!

But where's the one
I love the best,
even more
than all the rest?

Hello, Mum.
Hello, Little Fish.

Kiss, kiss, kiss,
hooray for fish!

Lucy Cousins

is the multi-award-winning creator of much-loved character Maisy.
She has written and illustrated over 100 books and has sold
over 25 million copies worldwide.

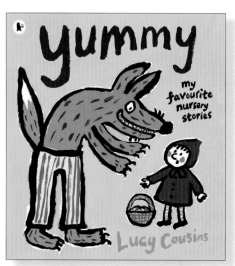

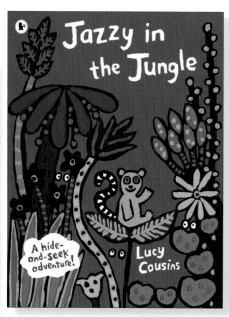

978-1-4063-2872-1

978-1-4063-4392-2

978-1-4063-3838-6

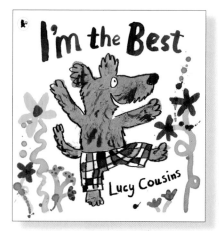

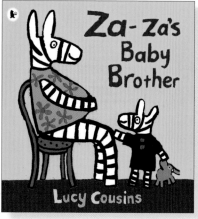

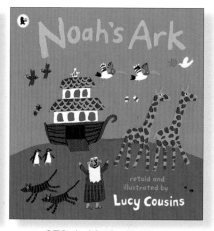

978-1-4063-2965-0

978-1-4063-3579-8

978-1-4063-4500-1

978-1-4063-4510-0

Available from all good booksellers

www.walker.co.uk